DEDICATED TO TERRY

Library of Congress Catalog Card Number: 82-083751. ISBN: 0-448-46625-2.

ONCE UPON A CAT

Edited by L. Savryn
Illustrated by Kathy Mitchell

Publishers
GROSSET & DUNLAP
New York

Puss in Boots

ONCE there was a poor miller whose sole worldly possessions were his mill, his donkey, and his cat. That was all he had to leave his three sons upon his death. So he called in no lawyer and made no will, but simply left the mill to the eldest, the donkey to the second, and the cat to the youngest.

The youngest son was quite downcast about his inheritance. "My brothers," he said to himself, "by putting their goods together will be able to earn an honest living. But though Puss may feed himself by catching mice, I shall certainly die of hunger."

Puss, who had guessed what his young master was thinking, began to speak. "Please, dear master, do not worry about your future. Give me a bag and a pair of boots, and you will soon see that you have a better bargain than you think."

As soon as Puss was provided with what he had asked for, he drew on his boots and, slinging the bag round his neck, trotted off to a neighboring warren in which he knew there was a great number of rabbits. He filled his bag with bran and weeds, laid it on the ground, and waited patiently till some simple young rabbit, unused to worldly snares and wiles, should see the dainty feast. Before long two thoughtless young rabbits caught at the bait and went headlong into the bag. The clever cat drew the strings and caught them.

Puss then went straight to the palace to see the king. Having been shown into the royal presence, he bowed and said, "Sire, I have been commanded to present these rabbits to Your Majesty by my lord, the Marquis of Carabas." (Such was the title the cat took it into his head to give the miller's son.)

"Tell your master that I am obliged by his courtesy, and that I accept his present with much pleasure," replied the king.

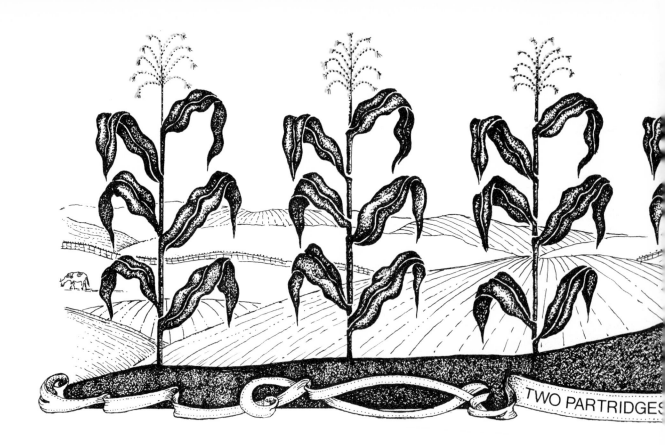

TWO PARTRIDGES

Later Puss went and hid himself in a cornfield and held his bag open as before. Soon two partridges were lured into the trap. Puss quickly drew the strings and made them both prisoners. Then he presented them to the king, as he had done with the rabbits. The king received the partridges very graciously and ordered the messenger to be rewarded for his trouble. For several months Puss continued to carry game to the king, always presenting it in the name of his master, the Marquis of Carabas.

One day Puss happened to hear that the king was going to take a drive along a riverbank, accompanied by his daughter, the most beautiful and charming princess in the world. He said to his master, "If you follow my advice, your fortune will be as good as made. You need only go and bathe in the river at the spot that I shall point out and leave the rest to me."

The miller's son did as his cat advised, and to be sure, the king came driving past. Puss began to bawl as loudly as he could, "Help! Help! The Marquis of Carabas is drowning!"

While the "marquis" was being fished out of the river by the king's attendants, Puss stepped up to the royal carriage. He told His Majesty that robbers had stolen his master's clothes—the

WERE LURED INTO THE TRAP

truth of the matter being that the cunning cat had hidden them
under a stone. The king immediately ordered one of his grooms
to go and fetch a handsome suit of purple and gold from the royal
wardrobe.

When the marquis, who was a handsome fellow, came forth
gaily dressed, he looked so elegant that the king took him for a
very fine gentleman, and the princess fell head over heels in love
with him. The king insisted on his getting into the carriage and
taking a drive with them.

Puss, highly delighted at the turn things were taking and
determined that all should turn out in the very best way, now ran
on before the carriage. When he reached a meadow where some
peasants were mowing the grass, he hurried up to them. "I say,
good folk," he cried, "if you do not tell the king when he comes
this way that the field you are mowing belongs to the Marquis of
Carabas, you shall all be chopped to bits!"

When the carriage passed by, the king put his head out and
asked the mowers whose good grassland that was. "It belongs to
the Marquis of Carabas, please Your Majesty," they said breath-
lessly, for the cat's threats had frightened them mightily.

"Upon my word, Marquis," said the king, "that is a fine estate you have."

"Yes, Sire," replied the marquis with an easy air. "It yields me a tolerable income every year."

Puss, who continued to run on before the carriage, soon came upon some reapers. "I say, you reapers," cried he, "mind you tell the king that this corn belongs to the Marquis of Carabas, or else you shall all be chopped into mincemeat!"

The king passed by a moment after and inquired to whom the cornfields belonged. "To the Marquis of Carabas, please Your Majesty," replied the reapers.

"Faith, it pleases me right well to see the beloved marquis is so wealthy!" said the king.

Puss kept running on before the carriage and repeating the same instructions to all the laborers he met, and the king was astounded at the vast possessions of the Marquis of Carabas. He kept congratulating the marquis, while the newly-made noble-man received each fresh compliment more lightly than the last, so that one could see he really was a marquis, and a very grand one, too.

At length Puss reached a magnificent castle belonging to an ogre, who was immensely rich, since all the lands the king had been riding through were a portion of his estate. Puss inquired what sort of a person the ogre might be and what he was able to do. Then he sent in a message asking leave to speak with the ogre, adding that he was unwilling to pass so near his castle without paying his respects to him. The ogre received Puss as civilly as it is in the nature of an ogre to do.

"I have been told," said Puss, "that you have the power of transforming yourself into all sorts of animals, such as a lion or an elephant."

"So I have," replied the ogre sharply. "Do you doubt it? Look, and you shall see me become a lion at once."

When Puss suddenly saw a lion before him, he was seized with such a fright that he scrambled up to the roof, although it was no easy job, owing to his boots. When the ogre had returned to his natural shape, Puss came down again and confessed he had been frightened.

"I have also been told," added Puss, "only I really cannot believe it, that you also possess the power of taking the shape of the smallest animals, and that you could change yourself into a rat or a mouse. But that is surely impossible."

"Impossible, indeed!" cried the ogre. "You shall see."

So saying, the ogre took on the shape of a mouse and began running about on the ground. Puss immediately pounced upon him and gobbled him up.

By this time the king had reached the gates of the ogre's magnificent castle. Puss, hearing the rumbling of the carriage across the drawbridge, ran out to meet the king, crying, "Your Majesty is welcome to the castle of the Marquis of Carabas."

"What! My dear Marquis," exclaimed the king, "does this castle also belong to you? Really, I never saw anything more splendid than the courtyard and the surrounding buildings. Pray let us see if the inside is equal to the outside."

The marquis gracefully helped the princess out of the carriage. Following the king, they mounted a flight of steps and were ushered by Puss into a vast hall, where they found an elegant feast waiting for them.

The king was positively delighted. The castle was magnificent, and the Marquis of Carabas was such an excellent young man. Furthermore, the princess was clearly in love with him. So, after drinking five or six glasses of wine, His Majesty hemmed and hawed and then said, "You have only to say the word, Marquis, to become my son-in-law."

The marquis bowed and looked tenderly at the princess. They were married the very next day. Puss, who had brought it all about, lived ever afterward as a great lord and hunted mice for mere sport whenever he pleased.

The Owl and the Pussycat

The Owl and the Pussycat went to sea
　　In a beautiful pea-green boat:
They took some honey and plenty of money
　　Wrapped up in a five-pound note.
The Owl looked up to the stars above,
　　And sang to a small guitar,
"O lovely Pussy, O Pussy, my love,
　　What a beautiful Pussy you are,
　　　You are,
　　　You are!
What a beautiful Pussy you are!"

Pussy said to the Owl, "You elegant fowl,
    How charmingly sweet you sing!
Oh! let us be married; too long we have tarried:
    But what shall we do for a ring?"
They sailed away for a year and a day,
    To the land where the bong-tree grows;
And there in a wood a Piggy-wig stood,
    With a ring at the end of his nose,
        His nose,
        His nose,
    With a ring at the end of his nose.

"Dear Pig, are you willing to sell for one shilling
    "Your ring?" Said the Piggy, "I will."
So they took it away, and were married next day
    By the Turkey who lives on the hill.
They dined on mince and slices of quince,
    Which they ate with a runcible spoon;
And hand in hand, on the edge of the sand,
    They danced by the light of the moon,
        The moon,
        The moon,
They danced by the light of the moon.

Edward Lear

Dick Whittington
and His Cat

IN long ago England there lived a poor boy named Dick Whittington who lost his parents when he was quite young. Having neither home nor friends, he decided to go to London and seek his fortune, for he had heard that the streets of the city were paved with gold. So he put his belongings into a bundle, tucked his faithful cat under his arm, and started on his journey.

Hour after hour Dick trudged along until he was quite worn out. Nobody knows how he continued to get food on the road—nor how he could walk so far, for it was a long way—nor what he did at night for a place to sleep in. Nevertheless, Dick Whittington reached London safely.

But, alas, once there he found the streets paved with hard stones covered with mud, and no gold was to be seen. He wandered about friendless and forlorn, for everybody was much too busy to heed a starving boy.

LORD MAYOR OF LONDON

At last he came to rest at the doorstep of a rich merchant. When the master of the house, Master Fitzwarren, returned home, he was touched with pity at the boy's miserable condition. He ordered the cook to take him in and give him food, adding that he might stay there and do such work for her as he was able.

Now, indeed, Dick might have been happy had it not been for the ill-usage of the cook, a most hard-hearted, ill-natured woman who knocked him about unmercifully. She treated him so badly that the merchant's daughter interfered and tried to protect him, for she felt very sorry for the lonely lad.

One day the merchant called his servants together, and told them that he had a ship ready to sail to foreign parts, and that each of them might venture something in her: whatever they sent should pay neither freight nor custom, and they should have fully all it sold for. The merchant's daughter noticed that young Dick Whittington was not there and ordered him to be called.

"But I have nothing to venture," said Dick sadly, "nothing but my faithful cat."

"Fetch thy cat, then, boy," said the merchant, "and send her!" Now, Dick was fond of the little creature and did not want to part with her. However, he obeyed his master and, with tears in his eyes, gave Puss to the captain of the ship.

But after this poor Dick's life became more and more intolerable, for the cook was constantly beating him. At last he felt he could endure it no longer and made up his mind to run away. He got up one morning very early and, making up the few things he possessed into a tiny bundle, he slipped unseen out of the house. He trudged as far as a place called Highgate and there sat down on a stone to rest. And as he so sat, the bells of Bow Church began ringing in the distance, and as they chimed it seemed to Dick that their sounds made a rhyme which ran thus in his ear:

"Turn again, Whittington,
Thrice Lord Mayor of London."

"Lord Mayor of London," he said to himself. "What one would endure to be Lord Mayor of London! But if I run away I'll never have a chance!" So he hurried home as fast as his legs would carry him, and he luckily got into the house before the cook was about.

While all this was happening in London, the ship that carried Dick's cat had made its way to the coast of Barbary, which was inhabited by Moors. These people received the captain and his crew kindly and were anxious to see what the strangers had in their ship. The captain, hoping to trade with them, sent some samples of his goods to the king of the country, who lived about a mile from the sea. The king was so well pleased that he invited the captain and his officers to come to his palace. Here the Englishmen were seated on rich carpets according to custom and, the king and queen being seated at the upper end of the apartment, dinner was brought in. But as soon as the dishes were put down, an immense number of rats and mice rushed out from every side and, swarming over the food, devoured it in an instant.

At this the captain and his men were much amazed, and the latter asked the royal couple if they did not find these vermin very offensive.

"Indeed, we do!" they replied.

"Then why suffer it?" inquired one young officer.

"Suffer it!" they exclaimed. "But how are we to prevent it? We would give the worth of half our kingdom to know of a remedy."

At this the captain thought of Dick's cat and immediately told the king he had a little animal on board his ship who would make short work of these disagreeable creatures.

"Send for this wonderful animal!" cried the king. "And if what you say as to its power proves true, I will load your ship with gold and jewels in exchange for her."

"Oh, but I do not know if we can spare her altogether," said the captain, "for then we in the ship will be overrun with rats and mice as you are. But, however, to oblige Your Majesty, I will fetch her for you to see."

"Oh, do, do!" exclaimed the queen, who had listened to all that passed. "I am all impatience to see this wonder."

Off hurried one of the ship's officers, while another meal was being prepared. He returned with Puss just as the rats and mice were busy eating that also. Down among them he put her, and she flew round, killing a great number, while the rest scuttled away in dismay at the appearance of this new and terrible foe.

Great was the joy of the king and queen to see their enemies thus dispersed, and the queen desired that the cat might be brought near so that she could pet her. The queen stroked Pussy's fur, and the cat curled herself round in the queen's lap and purred herself to sleep.

The king was so delighted with all this that he bargained with the captain for the whole of the ship's cargo and then gave him ten times as much for the cat! So, their business concluded, the captain and his men took farewell of the king and queen and, hoisting their sails, went with a fair wind to England, where we, too, must return.

One morning very early, the merchant had gone to his counting house to arrange his business for the day, when he was surprised by someone tapping at the door.

"Who's there?" he said.

"A friend," was the answer.

"What friend can come at this unseasonable hour?" exclaimed the merchant.

"A real friend is never unseasonable," replied the voice, "and I come to bring you news of the prosperous voyage of your good ship the *Unicorn*."

Up jumped the merchant in such joy that he quite forgot his gout. He opened the door, and there stood the captain with a cabinet of jewels.

"What have you there?" asked the merchant, seeing the cabinet.

"Why, this is the price of Whittington's cat!" answered the captain, and then he related the story of the rats and mice and showed the merchant the jewels of immense value that the King of the Moors had given in exchange for Puss.

"But, indeed," added the captain, "the treasure is too great for so poor a boy."

"Heaven forbid that I should deprive him of a farthing of it," cried the honest merchant. "Go, fetch the lad at once that we may tell him of his good fortune."

Now, Dick was busy about his usual morning work, and when he was summoned he was very unwilling to appear in his soiled clothes. But he had to obey, and when at last he entered the room the merchant bade him be seated.

Dick stared round in astonishment, and then, thinking they were making sport of him, begged his master not to mock a poor simple fellow, but let him go about his business. But the merchant took him by the hand and said kindly, "Indeed, I am in earnest, and I have sent for you to congratulate you on your good fortune, for your cat brought you more money than I possess in all the world, and may you live long to enjoy it!"

At last, being shown the jewels and assured they were all his, Dick fell on his knees and thanked Heaven, who had taken such care of a poor boy. He then entreated his master to accept the treasure, but the merchant refused. So Dick had to content himself with liberally rewarding the captain and all the ship's crew, as well as making presents to all the servants, not even excepting the cross-grained cook.

Now, indeed, did a happy time come to Dick. The merchant invited him to remain in his house till he could procure one for his own; the barber and the tailor were sent for, and when Dick left their hands, with his hair cut and curled and clad in a rich suit, he proved such a handsome fellow that the merchant's daughter straightway fell in love with him, as he indeed had loved her all along for her kindness and compassion to him. The merchant was nothing loath to have so wealthy a son-in-law, and before long the two young people were married. At the ceremony were present the Lord Mayor and all the eminent merchants of London.

But what is not less strange than what has hitherto been related is the fact that the prophecy that Bow Bells rang in the ears of the ragged boy sitting on his stone at Highgate came true. Three times was Richard Whittington made Lord Mayor of London. In the last year of his mayoralty it fell to him to entertain King Henry V and his queen on their return from France, and so splendid was the reception given them that the king conferred on Dick the honor of knighthood. It was on this occasion that the king looked round on the magnificence of the banquet and, marvelling at the wealth displayed, exclaimed, "Never, surely, did king have such a subject!"

"Nay," replied Whittington, "never surely did subject have such a king!"

So Sir Richard Whittington and his wife lived long and happily and died at a good old age, leaving worthy children to succeed them. All his life Dick showed great charity and daily fed many poor citizens, remembering how he had wandered hungry and forlorn about the streets as a boy. He built a church and college with maintenance for poor scholars and also a hospital for the sick; so that the memory of Dick Whittington and his cat should ever be held in honor by the citizens of London Town.

The White Cat

ONCE upon a time there was a king who, though he was growing old, did not at all wish to give up the government of his kingdom while he could still manage it very well. But this very same king had three sons, all handsome, brave, and noble of heart. And as these three princes were of an age when a young man wishes to know his place in life, the king thought it best to occupy the minds of his sons with promises that he could always get out of when the time came for keeping them.

So the king sent for his children and said: "As I am thinking of spending the rest of my life in the country, it seems to me that a pretty little dog would be very good company for me. Therefore, without any regard for your ages, I promise that the one who brings me the smallest and most beautiful dog shall succeed me at once. Prepare to leave at sunrise tomorrow, and let us meet at the same hour, in the same place, after a year has passed."

The three princes set off on their travels, promising to be friends always, never to be parted by envy or jealousy. Each took a different road. And although it is customary to tell of the adventures of either the eldest or the youngest son, it is about the middle son that you are going to hear. He was not only young and gay and handsome, but he knew everything a prince ought to know; and as for his courage, there was simply no end to it.

He journeyed from day to day, until one stormy evening he reached a great gloomy forest. Since he did not know his way, he took the first path he could find. He saw a faint light and began to make his way to what he hoped would be a cottage where he might find shelter for the night. But instead of coming upon a cottage, the prince found himself at the door of a magnificent castle.

The castle door was made of pure gold and covered with diamonds. In the middle of the door hung a deer's foot fastened to a chain of sapphires. The prince pulled the deer's foot and immediately the door flew open. All that the prince could see were twelve pairs of hands, each holding a torch. As he entered a hall paved with lapis lazuli, two lovely voices sang:

"The hands you see floating above
   Will swiftly your bidding obey;
If your heart dreads not conquering love,
   In this place you may fearlessly stay."

This welcome made it clear to the prince that the palace was enchanted. He allowed the mysterious hands to guide him toward a door of coral, which opened into a vast hall of mother-of-pearl. He passed through this hall into a number of other rooms, glittering with thousands of lights and full of beautiful pictures and precious things. After he had passed through sixty apartments, all equally splendid, the hands led him to the most magnificent room of all, upon the walls of which were painted the histories of Puss in Boots and a number of other famous cats. There was a table set for supper with two golden plates, and golden spoons and forks. The prince was wondering who the second place could be for, when a door opened and in came a tiny figure not a foot high. It had a long black veil and was escorted by two cats wearing black capes and carrying swords.

The prince thought he must be dreaming; but the little figure came up to him and threw back its veil, and he saw an incredibly lovely white cat. She looked very young and melancholy, and in a voice that went straight to his heart, she said:

"Welcome, Prince. Your presence here pleases me."

The prince bowed. "Madam," he replied, "I thank you for receiving me so kindly. But surely you are no ordinary cat. Indeed, the way you speak and the splendor of your castle prove it plainly."

"I beg you to spare me these compliments," said the white cat, and she commanded the meal to be served.

The prince dared not ask any more questions for fear of displeasing the pretty little creature. So as the mysterious hands began to bring in all sorts of delicacies, the prince began to talk about other things and found that his hostess was interested in all the subjects he cared for himself; she talked with him of state affairs, of theaters, of fashions. When the night was far advanced, the white cat wished the prince good night. The hands conducted him to his bedchamber, a most unusual room hung with tapestry worked with butterflies' wings of every color.

In the morning the prince was awakened by the hands and presented with a hunting costume. All the cats who lived in the castle were assembled in the courtyard, for the white cat was going out hunting. The prince was to ride a richly bridled wooden horse. The white cat herself was riding a monkey. Never was there a pleasanter hunting party, and when they returned to the palace, the prince and the white cat dined together as before.

And so the days passed, in every kind of amusement, until the year was nearly gone. The prince did not concern himself with the little dog he was seeking for the king and only found time to think how happy he was to be with the white cat!

But one morning the white cat said to the prince, "Do you know that you have only three days left to look for the little dog for your father? Your brothers have already found lovely ones."

"What can have made me forget such an important thing?" the prince cried. "My whole fortune depends upon it; and even if I could in such a short time find a dog pretty enough to gain me a kingdom, where should I find a horse who could carry me all that way in three days?" And he began to be very anxious, indeed.

But the white cat said to him, "My friend, do not trouble yourself. I will make everything easy for you. Tomorrow the good wooden horse will take you to your country in twelve hours."

"I thank you, beautiful cat," said the prince, "but what good will it do me to get back if I do not have a dog to take to my father?"

"See here," answered the white cat, holding up an acorn to the prince's ear. "There is a prettier one in this than in the dog star."

The prince listened and inside the acorn he heard the barking of a little dog. He thanked the cat a thousand times and said goodbye quite sadly when the time came for him to set out.

"The days have passed so quickly with you," he said, "I only wish I could take you with me now."

But the white cat shook her head and sighed deeply in answer.

When the prince arrived at his father's palace, the sound of trumpets announced his return. His two brothers were already inside presenting their dogs to the king, and nobody could decide which was the prettier. Then the prince stepped forward, drawing from his pocket the acorn the white cat had given him. He opened it quickly, and there upon a white cushion was a little dog who got up at once and began to dance. The king did not know what to say, for it was impossible for anything to be more lovely or more remarkable.

Nevertheless, as he was in no more hurry to part with his crown than he was a year ago, the king told his sons that he would ask them to go once again and take another year to seek by land and sea a piece of muslin so fine that it could be drawn through the eye of a needle.

The prince mounted the wooden horse and in a short time arrived at the palace of his beloved white cat, who received him with greatest joy.

"How could I hope that you would come back to me, my prince?" she said. And then he stroked and petted her and told her of his successful journey and how he had come back to ask her help, as he believed that it was impossible to find what the king demanded.

"Rest easy, king's son," said she, "there are cats in this castle who will be quite able to spin you the cloth you require. So you have nothing to do but to give me the pleasure of your company while it is making."

And so the days passed as before. The prince and the white cat watched displays of fireworks, hunted, and dined on succulent dishes. As the white cat frequently gave proofs of an excellent understanding, the prince was by no means tired of her company. When the prince was alone, he wondered how it could be possible that a small white cat could be endowed with all the attractions of the very best and most charming of women.

Before the year had passed the cat reminded the prince of his duty to his father:

"This time," she said, "you will travel to your homeland in a superb chariot of gold drawn by twelve snow-white horses. And

when you appear before the king in such glory he surely will not refuse you the crown that you deserve. Take this walnut. In it you will find the piece of muslin your father asked for."

"Lovely cat," said the prince, "how can I thank you properly for all your kindness to me? Only tell me that you wish it, and I will give up forever all thought of being king and will stay here with you always."

"Dear friend," she replied, "it shows the goodness of your heart that you should care so much for a little white cat, but you must not stay."

So the prince kissed her little paw and set out. This time he was so late that his brothers did not think he would arrive in time. They had already displayed their pieces of muslin to the king proudly. But the king, who was only too glad to make a difficulty, sent for a particular needle, which was kept among the crown jewels and had such a small eye that everybody saw at once that it was impossible for the muslin to pass through it. The brothers were angry and were beginning to complain that it was a trick,

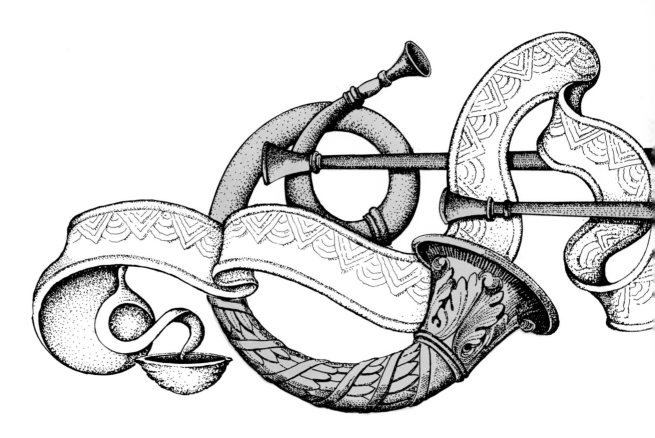

when suddenly the trumpets sounded and the prince came in. He greeted his father and brothers, took the walnut from his pocket and opened it, and drew out of it a piece of muslin four hundred ells long, woven with the loveliest colors and most wonderful patterns; and when the needle was brought it went through the eye six times with the greatest of ease! The king turned pale and the other princes stood silent and sorrowful, for nobody could deny that this was the most marvelous piece of muslin that was to be found in the world.

Presently the king turned to his sons and said with a deep sigh:

"Nothing could comfort me more in my old age than your willingness to obey my wishes. Go then once more, and whoever at the end of a year can bring back the loveliest princess shall be married to her, for my successor must certainly be married, a king must have a queen."

The prince considered that he had earned the kingdom twice over, but he was too well bred to argue about it. So he returned to the white cat faster than he had come. This time she was expecting him. The path to her palace was strewn with flowers and lined with a thousand burning torches.

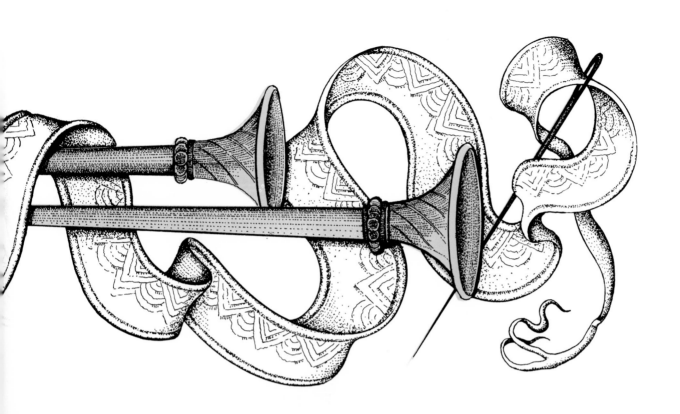

"Well," she said, "here you are once more, without a crown."

"Dear Blanchette," said he, "thanks to you, I have earned one twice over; but since my father is so unwilling to part with his throne, there would be no pleasure in taking it."

"Never mind," she answered. "As you must take back a lovely princess with you next time, I will be on the lookout for one for you."

So the time slipped away even more pleasantly than before. When only one day remained of the year, the white cat said to the prince that if he wanted to take a lovely princess home with him, he must be prepared to do as she told him.

"Take your sword," she said, "and cut off my head!"

"I!" cried the prince. "I cut off your head! How could I do it?"

"You must do as I tell you," she replied.

Tears came into the prince's eyes as he drew his sword and, with a trembling hand, cut off the little white head. Imagine his astonishment when suddenly a lovely princess stood before him. While he was still speechless with amazement, the door opened and a company of lords and ladies entered, each carrying a cat's skin. They all rejoiced at being returned to their natural shapes.

"You see, my dear friend," said the princess, "you were right in supposing me to be no ordinary cat. My father was the ruler of six kingdoms. He tenderly loved my mother, who fell gravely ill a short time before my birth. Alas, the court physicians despaired of saving her life, and sorcerers and wizards were summoned from distant lands to try and restore her to health.

"One night a tiny, ugly old woman appeared before the castle gates demanding to see the king. She was one of a number of fairies who tended a garden where magical fruits with wondrous healing powers grew in great abundance. These wicked fairies were willing to send as much of their fruit as could be carried away by two hundred camels, but there was one condition: The king and queen must give the fairies their child as soon as it should be born. Since my mother was so very near death, my father consented to the cruel bargain, lest he lose both his wife and his child.

"The fairies took me to a tower, where I grew up surrounded by everything beautiful and learned everything that is ever taught to a princess. My only playmates were a parrot and a little dog, who both could talk. I was even allowed to wander in a delightful garden, in which bloomed every sort of flower and fruit.

"I should have remained very happy, if not for a visit from one of the old fairies, who came mounted upon a dragon. She informed me that my wedding day was drawing near and that I should prepare to become the bride of the king of the dwarfs. You can imagine my horror at being betrothed to a being as cruel as he was ugly.

"I was determined to escape. The fairies always supplied me with flax for my spinning, and I made enough cord for a ladder that would reach to the foot of my tower. Alas! My plan was discovered by the crossest of the old fairies. She was so furious with me that she changed me into a white cat. Then I was brought here, and I found all the lords and ladies of my father's court had been changed into cats, and all the servants were invisible, except for their hands.

"The fairies warned me that this enchantment could only be brought to an end if by some impossible turn of fate I could persuade a young and handsome prince who loved me to cut off my head."

"And he has done so, lovely and clever princess," interrupted the prince, throwing himself at her feet. "And if you care for me as much as I care for you, then do consent to marry me."

"I already love you better than anyone in the world," the princess said, "but now it is time to go back to your father and we shall hear what he says about it."

So the prince gave her his hand, and they set out in the golden chariot. The prince and princess reached the palace just as the other two princes arrived with two beautiful princesses. For the third time, the trumpets sounded and the courtiers announced his sons' arrival to the king.

"Are the ladies beautiful?" he asked anxiously.

And when they answered that nobody had ever before seen such lovely princesses he seemed quite annoyed. However, he received them all graciously, but found it impossible to choose one of them as being the most beautiful. Seeing that the king was in a bit of a difficulty, Blanchette stepped forward and said:

"It is a pity that Your Majesty, who is so capable of governing, should think of retiring. I already have six kingdoms—permit me to bestow one upon you and upon your youngest and eldest sons, and to enjoy the remaining three in the society of your second son. And may it please Your Majesty to keep your own kingdom and make no decision concerning the beauty of the three princesses, who, without such a proof of Your Majesty's preference, will no doubt live happily together!"

The king and all the courtiers could not conceal their joy and astonishment, and the marriage of the three princes was celebrated at once. The festivities lasted several months, and then each king and queen lived happily ever after.

The Cat and the Mouse in Partnership

A CERTAIN cat, having made the acquaintance of a certain mouse, spoke so much of the great friendship she felt for her that they decided to keep house together.

"But we must provide for the winter or else we shall go hungry," said the cat.

So the cat and mouse bought a little pot of fat, but they did not know where to put it. Finally the cat said:

"I know of no place where it could be better stored than in the church. No one will trouble to take it away from there. We will hide it in a corner, and we won't touch it until we need it."

So the little pot was placed in safety; but soon the cat had a great longing for it and said to the mouse:

"I wanted to tell you, little mouse, that my cousin has asked me to stand godmother to her little son, who is white with brown spots. Let me go out today, and do you take care of the house alone."

"Yes, go certainly," replied the mouse, "and when you eat anything good, think of me. I should very much like a drop of the red christening wine."

But it was all untrue. The cat had no cousin and had not been asked to stand godmother. She went to the church, straight to the little pot of fat, and licked the top off. Then she took a walk on the roofs of the town, looked at the view, stretched herself out in the sun, and licked her lips whenever she thought of the little pot of fat. As soon as it was evening she went home again.

"Ah, here you are!" said the mouse. "You must certainly have had an enjoyable day."

"It went off very well," answered the cat.

"What was the child's name?" asked the mouse.

"Top-off," said the cat dryly.

"Top-off!" echoed the mouse, "what a curious name."

"It is no worse than Breadthief, as your godchild is called," said the cat.

It was long after this that another great longing came over the cat. So she said to the mouse:

"You must again be kind enough to look after the house alone, for I have been asked a second time to stand godmother, and as this child has a white ring round its neck, I cannot refuse."

The kind mouse agreed; and the cat crept under the town wall to the church and ate up half of the pot of fat. When she came home the mouse asked:

"What was this child called?"

"Half-gone," answered the cat.

"Half-gone! What a name! I have never heard it in my life."

Soon the cat's mouth began to water once more after her licking business.

"All good things in threes," she said to the mouse. "I have again been asked to stand godmother. The child is quite black and has very white paws, but not a single white hair on its body. This only happens once in two years, so do let me go out."

"Top-off, Half-gone," murmered the mouse. "Such names make me very thoughtful."

That night when the cat came home sleek and satisfied, the mouse asked at once after the third child's name.

"It won't please you any better," said the cat, "he was called All-gone."

"All-gone!" repeated the mouse. "That name is as peculiar as the others. All-gone! What can it mean?" She shook her head, curled herself up, and went to sleep.

From this time on, no one asked the cat to stand godmother, but when the winter came and there was nothing to be got outside, the mouse said:

"Come, Cat, we will go to our pot of fat that we have stored away; it will taste very good."

"Yes, indeed," thought the cat, "it will taste as good to you as if you stretched your thin tongue out of the window."

They started off, and when they reached the church they found the pot in its place, but quite empty!

"Ah," said the mouse, "now I know what has happened! You were never asked to stand godmother at three christenings. Instead, you came to the church three times to eat up our pot of fat. First you licked the top off, the second time half of it was gone, then…"

"Will you be quiet!" screamed the cat. "Another word and I will eat you up."

"All-gone" was already on the poor mouse's tongue, and scarcely was it out than the cat made a spring at her, seized and swallowed her.

You see, with cats and mice, that is the way of the world.